Josephine
and the
Sheep of Dreams

Caroline Louise Altman

ISBN: 0692433473
ISBN-13: 978-0692433478

Cover logo design by Cathy Barragan

TO THE MUSIC IN THE TREES

This book, like the musical, is dedicated to the small voices, the lofty dreams, the vibrant colors, and those who see them and choose them everyday.

In Memory of My Mother, Virginia McBride Altman
1935-2003

CONTENTS

ACKNOWLEDGMENTS

Many thanks to the dedicated cast of actors and singers that brought *Josephine and the Sheep of Dreams,* the musical to fruition, in its premiere on May 2, 2015. Thanks also to the Children's Creativity Museum Theater for its support and nurturing of this venture. And a big thank you to my supportive friends, family, and husband, Matt.

1.

JOSEPHINE stared at the dark sky from her bedroom window. She pulled her hair into a loose bun on top of her head, and took in the sparkling pinpoints of light that broke up the darkness.

She took out her journal and reread last night's entry:

Oh—to live in the space and time before you fall asleep. That tasty little threshold where the heaviness of the real world slips away and the dream can begin.

The dream! Full of imaginative quirks and cozy nuzzles and fretless adventure.

The sky is alive with a million sparkles of magic sand that twinkle in the moonlight.

A thousand tiny stars that sing like a music box, and flitter like fairy wings.

Curled up in her blue and lavender quilt on her bed, a familiar melody from her childhood flooded her consciousness, and humming away, she began to count. *One...two...three...four...*

Star light, star bright, first star I see tonight, I wish I may, I wish I might, have this wish I wish tonight.

Sixteen...seventeen...eighteen...nineteen...

Every night she counted the stars. Her mother was out there, she was sure.

When Mama passed away last year, she told her to look for her in the stars. The request was wrapped up in one of the extraordinary stories of delight that Josephine and her mother would create together each night before bed, or in the airport waiting for a flight, or on long car rides to pass the time. The stories were fantastical and brought color and light into a world that Josephine otherwise found drab. Then Mama was gone. And so were the stories.

Twenty...twenty-one...twenty two...

"Josephine! Are you awake? Have you finished your homework?"

Dad called to her from behind her closed door, "Or are you counting the stars? You cannot afford another incomplete. Write your essay."

Josephine, startled out of her counting trance, examined the notebook at her side. The assignment was to write an essay. Not a fun creative writing project, not a story with clever irony, or mystical powers. This was to "Write an objective and realistic modern essay based on fact ,in the form of a letter to someone far away." A way to glorify all the things that Josephine found dull and colorless.

She sighed and called back to her father, "Yes, Dad. I'm doing it now."

Thirty-eight...thirty-nine...forty. Stop. Write the essay.

DEAR FAR, FAR AWAY PERSON,

there was once a ~~Princess~~, girl who lived in ~~a flowering meadow of light and~~ the suburbs with her ~~mom and~~ dad ~~because her mom had... her mom had... she looked for her mother in the stars every night~~ and they missed her mom everyday. Dad missed her laugh and the girl missed...all the stories. All the stories. And she wished she were here.

Forty-one...forty-two...forty-three.

Josephine turned the page.

DEAR STRANGER,

Life for a teenager in today's world is simple. Modern conveniences, medicine, fresh air, food and water have made life easy. If you fall in line. If you stick to the rules...

She began to hum and tap on her notebook with her pencil in a martial rhythm...

There's a path all laid out I know it.
And some say never stray from the path.
But the path all laid out, as I know it,
Seems so fixed, so straight, go to school,
Don't be late, get a job, get a date.
Do not question, it's just fate.
Wrapped in a good strong bow.
But what of the dreamer that guides us from dark to light?
What of the dreamer that sings in the night?

Josephine looked at her paragraph and laughed to herself, "I am a crazy person."

She picked up the photograph in the frame by her bed, and looked at the familiar image of her mother. Soft, thoughtful eyes hiding a slight smirk of mischief.

"Yes, you must find this funny. Me with writer's block." She quipped to the photograph.

"You don't know the half of it," she added.

She went back to her notebook and began to write.

DEAR MAMA,

I am counting the stars. Dear Mama, wishing you weren't so far up above me. Mama, take my hand and say you love me and I'll be okay.

She tore the page out of her book and folded the letter. Placing it gently under her pillow, she lay back and looked out the window again at the stars and the vast darkness. She wanted to sleep; she wanted to dream and let imagination take flight. Her mind raced in a silent prayer:

Little whispers break the silence like thunder and colors so vivid in my mind at night. In my dream I don't follow directions, in my dream all the craziness makes sense. Ghosts and visions rise to offer me protection, wild thoughts no longer trapped inside a fence. My thoughts seem clear within their haze. Someday I hope the strength I find at nighttime will catch up with who I am during the days.

She closed her eyes. She wished she could sleep...

Just then she was startled by the sound of small horn. Josephine sat up and looked around, and figuring it was just a noise from the neighbors, settled herself again on her pillow, and turned off the light.

Then it began again, and as she peered through the darkness, she saw furry creatures of fluff come tumbling one, by one, into her bedroom window!

They appeared to be tiny sheep! Each had a number affixed to its back, and one had a rose in its teeth!

They seemed to be assembling into some sort of military formation around her bed, and once they were all together, the one with the horn raised his hoof and gave a deep bow with great flourish.

Josephine started to address them, "Um...I'm not sure—"

"BAAAAA!" they all shouted back as if trying to shut her up.

The leader with the horn stepped forward.

"I am One!" he declared.

"One what?" Josephine questioned.

"Just One!" he replied.

"Just one what?" she asked, "Just one

sheep?"

"Not *just one sheep*! ONE! Master and Commander of all the Counting Sheep!"

And with that, Josephine noticed the little bib on his back had the number "1" on it. She began to count the others,

"One, two, three, four—"

This was all the intro the sheep seemed to need, for at once they launched into a very complicated song and dance that ranged in feel from a high school pep squad to a dangerous and refined Cuban Tango.

There is a way to bring sleep your way—
It starts with One, Two, Three Four
(that's us!)
Keep counting more, you'll find us such a bore,
Oh sheep are the way to sleep.
Oh sheep! You count the sheep
As we leap through the air with glee!
A lamb, sometimes a ram,
And we do it all for ewe!
Oh sheep! You'll fall asleep!

A woolly sedative
With meditative charm.
We'll guide you into slumber
And run back to the farm.
Baa Baa Baa Baa!

By the time the sheep finished their routine, Josephine had fallen into an angelic slumber. Quite pleased with themselves, they did several quick hoof high fives, and then leapt out the window as silently as they had entered.

Josephine tossed and turned. The breeze from the open window caused the little hairs around her face to tickle her forehead. She stirred and caught the shadow of yet another visitor who had landed in her bedroom.

Sleepily she eyed the graceful fairylike lady across the room. She sat up with a start.

"Mama?" she whispered across the dark

room.

The lady froze and then slowly turned right and left as if looking for another person in the room.

"Um, no...I'm not Mama," she mumbled, cautiously, "You should be asleep. And why can you see me?" she continued.

"You are right in front of me, Mama. Have you come back for a story?" asked Josephine.

"Listen," began the lady, "I am afraid I am not who you think I am. I wish I was your mother, but I am the Tooth Fairy. I am here for your tooth. I believe it is a right incisor? So if you just hand it over, I'll give you a shiny silver dollar and just be on my way."

"Tooth Fairy?" asked Josephine, "I don't have any teeth for you. I am fourteen years old and lost my baby teeth long ago."

The lady was quite crestfallen.

"Oh, no." she began, "This is seems to be the story of my life. I suppose you have lost sight of wonder and magic as well?"

Before Josephine could answer, the lady began to sing a sweet lullaby:

All the children grow so quickly
I help them on their way.
My castle road is paved
With pearly white ones.
Mr. Sandman and I,
We look down on the children
And say, oh we say,
Little ones, Don't stop your play, little ones.
You can keep your childish wonder,
Wonder in the world as you grow up.
You can see the magic sprinkled with the tears.
And the laughter of that child so innocent and wild,
Offers comfort and contentment
through the years.

While moved by the sentiment and the lovely melody, Josephine was a little confused by the Tooth Fairy serenade.

"I'm not sure what you mean." She said.

"Well, I think sometimes people lose their sense of wonder as they grow up. *Objective realism* shouldn't keep you from counting the stars. It isn't one or the other." She explained.

"Nobody understands why I count the stars. I do it to keep track of my mother. To hold on," said Josephine.

The Tooth Fairy looked thoughtful.

"Hold on to yourself, Josephine, and she'll be with you. Don't lose your colors."

"Don't lose my what?" asked Josephine.

But it was too late. In an instant the lady was gone, and Josephine ran to the window to try to catch a final glimpse of her fleeing figure.

"This is very odd" she started to say when she was suddenly distracted by loud laughter behind her.

2.

WHEN JOSEPHINE turned around she was startled to discover that her bedroom had been transformed to her old 3rd grade classroom. Mr. Sand was there with his strict demeanor and piercing eyes, and she was standing in front of the class.

"Miss Josephine!" he barked, "Wake up! We can't wait all day. You are up next!"

Josephine was clueless.

"What?" she asked.

Mr. Sand sighed, "Would someone like to remind Josephine about the oral reports?"

"Worth 89% of your grade?" added snarky Mary.

"For the rest of your life!" continued little Sam in his best mocking voice.

Josephine remembered Sam and Mary, and was glad they had gone to another middle school. She was not happy to see them again.

"We're waiting!" Mr. Sand said, impatiently.

"Okay, okay. What's it on again?" Josephine asked in a small voice.

Mr. Sand rolled his eyes. "Lava flow through the Appalachian Mountains, and how it affects cotton candy sales at Disneyland."

"DUH!" chimed the whole class.

Josephine looked out at the sea of students that seemed to be multiplying before her eyes. The students, sensing her discomfort like a pack of wolves spotting a wounded deer, rose to their feet and approached her. They began to circle her with a malicious chant:

JOSEPHINE IS NOT PREPARED. JOSEPHINE IS NOT PREPARED. SHE'S TURNED WHITE AND NOW SHE'S SCARED 'CAUSE JOSEPHINE IS NOT PREPARED. JOSEPHINE IS NOT PREPARED. JOSEPHINE IS NOT PREPARED. SHE'S TURNED WHITE AND NOW SHE'S SCARED 'CAUSE JOSEPHINE IS NOT PREPARED!

"Okay!" shouted Josephine, and she decided to do her level best. Each time she stated a fact, one of the students would jump in and correct her.

She began, "The Appalachian Mountains are purple."

"They're pink!" shouted Tommy.

She continued, "...And covered with beautiful roses"

"That stink!" remarked Meredith.

Josephine grit her teeth. "There lives a wicked witch..."

"No it's the King of Spain," corrected Alex.

"He gardens in the sunlight?" she ventured.

"He dances in the rain!" All the students shouted. "She's wrong, wrong, wrong, wrong. She doesn't know her stuff. She's wrong, wrong, wrong, wrong! Oh we've heard quite enough!"

Josephine felt herself shrinking, and her face growing red. This was a nightmare. As if on cue all the students started to shout, "NIGHTMARE!"

The wild sound of thundering hooves ripped through the classroom, and Josephine ducked as a ghostlike horse went tearing by.

"Children! Children! Sit down!" shouted Mr. Sand. "Josephine, please continue...in Portuguese."

Josephine reeled. "Portuguese? But I don't know Portuguese!"

"Minus 250 points!" shouted Mr. Sand, "Go on!"

Josephine took a deep breath, "Now, cotton candy grows deep underground..."

"Like flowers!" interrupted Vanessa.

Josephine shot Vanessa a dirty look, and continued, "...And needs a climate dry and still and calm."

"Likes showers!" corrected Jeremy, smugly.

Josephine persevered, "IT'S STILL A TASTY TREAT..."

"To clean the bathroom sink," laughed Hillary.

"IT'S WORTH THE SIMPLE PRICE..."

Mr. Sand intervened, "Now Josephine, think!"

The students sprang to their feet, "She's wrong, wrong, wrong, wrong. She doesn't know her stuff. She's wrong, wrong, wrong, wrong! Oh we've heard quite enough!"

"She's wrong, wrong, wrong, wrong, wrong, wrong. What is she to do? Wrong, wrong, wrong, wrong, wrong, wrong, wrong!"

"And she's naked too!" Shouted Mary.

Josephine looked down and saw that, indeed, her clothes had vanished, and she was in front of the class in her underwear!

The thundering hooves went sweeping by once more and Josephine felt herself whisked away, transported through the dark sky at an alarming pace. She held on to the Nightmare with all her might—at least she was leaving the ridicule of the 3rd Grade!

3.

THE NIGHTMARE rode on for a while longer and Josephine began to adjust her eyes to the night sky. Luckily her clothing seemed to have returned to her, which was good because a chill had developed in the air.

They slowed to a trot, and finally to a slow walk, and when Josephine slid off the side of the immense animal, she found her feet on solid ground once again. Suddenly the horse rose on her hind legs with a great whinny, and cantered off toward the dark horizon. Josephine turned to see what had frightened the huge animal, and was surprised to see a small herd of sheep heading her way. They were running on their hind legs and shouting. Josephine recognized One, leading the pack with his small horn.

When the sheep saw Josephine they charged at her, and ducked behind her for protection. Confused, she looked up and saw that they were running from a small boy dressed in red and green, sporting a pointy hat, jingle bells, a black leather jacket and very hip shades.

The small boy was crying plaintively has he pursued the sheep, "Don't run away! Please help me get home! Please!"

He stopped momentarily when he saw Josephine and politely greeted her, "Oh, hello! And Merry Christmas!"

Then he stared up his wild chase again. The sheep made a break for it and the little boy darted after them.

"Wait!" cried Josephine.

The little boy froze. The sheep froze. All

eyes were on Josephine.

"What is going on? And did you just say *Merry Christmas*? You do realize that it's May, right?" asked Josephine.

The boy gave a big sigh. "Yes," he said, "I am Elvis Elf—*don't say it*—my mother was a fan. I said *Merry Christmas* because..." Elvis fought back a tear, "I'm not supposed to be lost..."

Josephine felt sorry and began to ask about his troubles but Elvis stopped her and said, "Let me just sing about it."

On cue the sheep circled Elvis and tiny rock and roll instruments materialized in their hooves. Josephine was impressed by their musicality. Elvis began:

Last Christmas all was swell.
We loaded up the sleigh.
The usual Noel
Did not turn out that way!
We were sailing through
The stars that night,
Santa was laughing

With all his might.
We hit a bump in the Milky Way
That sent me flyin' right outta the sleigh!
I fell out—right outta the sleigh.
For me there was no Christmas Day!
I fell out—right outta the sleigh,
And now I get down on my knees and pray!

It was time for the dance break, and Josephine felt her self pulled into and energetic rockabilly romp. As this was her first dance with livestock, she was happy to find she could keep up with their four feet while only on two feet herself. Dance break over, Elvis resumed:

I don't have any skills by being an elf,
And I miss Santa, all by myself.
Now all I need is to hitch a ride,
But all the reindeer just run and hide!

The song ended with a flourish (and a brief woolly guitar solo) and the flock congratulated itself on the impromptu gig.

Elvis turned to Josephine and said, "Do you get it now? I've just got to make it home!"

Josephine nodded, "So...why are you chasing sheep?"

"Reindeer, " corrected Elvis.

"No," Josephine turned to the sheep band, "You guys are sheep, right?"

"BAAAAAAA!" they agreed.

"Oh no," sighed Elvis, "This is terrible. You see, we don't have any sheep at the North Pole, and I thought they looked kinda cute and furry..."

One intervened, "It's okay Elvis. We will help you if you like. Fly with us!"

Elvis brightened, "Thank you, thank you very much!"

Josephine shouted after their retreating figures, "Wait! Sheep can't fly!"

One turned back to her and called, "Use your imagination!"

"What?" questioned Josephine.

"Imagination." Mr. Sand suddenly appeared before her.

He was tall and serious looking as usual, but had traded in his usual oxford shirt and khaki trousers for a long robe and wizard hat. He made a good wizard, actually, but Josephine was not happy to see him.

"Oh, it's you," she said. "Don't tell me you are encouraging me to imagine things! You and your oral reports. Facts. I'm not good at facts."

"Facts are important," he said.

"Yes, I know. I hear that everyday," she responded.

"But so is fiction. So is the story. It is a path," he added.

Josephine was not in the mood for his philosophy. "I know all about the path. I hear all the time about the places I am supposed to go. The right school, the right job, the right choices. The facts. But they don't seem to fit me. I feel that I am called by other things. By colors and magic."

"And that's okay too," he said.

"You know," started Josephine, "It doesn't seem to be okay. I am totally alone in my stories. I have no one to create with me, and I can't relate to what other people find important."

"Ah," he said, "It's all about balance, Josephine. All about listening to what's inside and what's outside, simultaneously."

"What does that even mean?"

Mr. Sand cleared his throat and as he open his arms wide, his large bell sleeves swept the ground like great wings. He started a speech.

You wish your life was just a dream,
But things aren't always what they seem.

You need to find a path that's true.
Following the heartbeat set by you.

"Set by me? Josephine asked.

"Shh—don't interrupt," continued Mr. Sand.

There's a time when you long
For adventure and dare,
And time when you're
Feeling alone and so scared,
But the world keeps you grounded
When you are aware
That asleep or awake
You breathe the same air.
Head in the clouds,
Feet on the earth
You'll feel sadness,
And you'll feel mirth.
The story was written
The day of your birth,
And eyes wide open,
You'll see your true worth.

Mr. Sand lowered his arms and closed his eyes in great reverence. Josephine wanted to speak but was unsure if it was appropriate. Suddenly his eyes popped open and the thundering of hooves could be heard passing above them. Josephine ducked as the horse flew by above their heads.

Mr. Sand watched the Nightmare go by and studied Josephine for a moment.

"Don't lose your colors, Josephine." And with that he was gone.

"Don't lose my—" Josephine was silenced by his exit.

As Mr. Sand ran towards the horizon his robe flew out behind him in great sheets of bright light. The glow was warm and seemed to wrap her in a blanket of tenderness and well being. She looked up to the skies and was overwhelmed by the display of colors she suddenly saw above her. A vivid spectrum stretched as far as she could see. Josephine gasped and whispered to herself what she could clearly read emblazoned on her heart:

Colors so bright, I see them all
Voices so sweet, from creatures small.
There's a glow that surrounds us.
I know it surrounds us.
Does no one see it too?
Where is the friend
To travel through creation?
Who can pretend
And laugh with animation?
I'm all alone in a world that seems grey.
Who will come wash the dullness away?
I seek a world
Where light is always shining.
Give me that world
With borders less defining.
Dreams give us hope
In a world that seems grey.
Someone come wash the dullness away.
So I can awake and dream in the day.

4.

JOSEPHINE!

"Are you alright?"

Josephine looked up see to see the Tooth Fairy in front of her.

"I still don't have a tooth for you," said Josephine.

The woman looked surprised.

"Of course not!" She said, "You are too old to be losing your baby teeth. I thought we might make up a story."

Josephine looked closer and the woman's features began to soften and glow.

"Mama?" she said, "Is that you?"

"Well, it's not the Tooth Fairy!" replied the woman, "Of course it's me."

Josephine was overcome with a wave of warm emotion and she rushed towards her mother.

"Oh Mama! How I've missed you. Oh Mama!" She cried.

"Don't be silly—I'm right here. What is the matter with you?"

"Is it really you? Can I touch you?" asked Josephine.

Her mother welcomed Josephine into her outstretched arms and they embraced for a long time. Josephine felt the softness of her mother's touch that she had long forgotten until this moment.

"Now," her mother said, holding her close to her, "What is going on that seems so troubling?

"Well, I don't have anyone anymore—since you went away. And I am trying to live in our stories, in our magical worlds, but no one will let me. Everyone keeps telling me to take my head out of the clouds."

Her mother looked at her thoughtfully.

"Then take your head out of the clouds." She said, "How can you see what is in front of you if you are always looking to the clouds?"

"But when I wake up, you'll be gone," said Josephine.

"Little girl, I won't be gone. I'll be with you always. Trust that I am with you, and reach out to the world around you. How do I put this? Shall I sing it to you?"

Josephine nodded.

Little girl, I'm in your heart and mind.
Little girl, just trust and you'll be fine.
There are places to explore all your days.
Open your eyes and discover lots of ways
To find color in the sea,
Music in the trees,
Laughter in the market,
Even your ABCs.
Look for twinkle in the eye,
Mischief in a grin,
Whistling on the sidewalk,
And that's just to begin.
All the wonder in the world
Is not just in your head.
When you journey through the world
Please remember what I've said.
Find the giggle in the stream,
Glances between friends,
Sunsets on the ocean,

You'll see there is no end
To the magic for the dreamer who awakes.

As she finished the last line of the song, Josephine's mother held up a small, sparkling star locket.

"Here," she said. "This will protect you. Now get to it. You have a dragon to fight."

"Dragon?" asked Josephine, "I didn't dream any dragon!"

"That's true, but your mother can be quite creative too. Go get 'em!" she laughed and suddenly disappeared.

Just as suddenly, a huge fiery creature materialized before Josephine, and she felt the weight of an invisible sword in her hand. Josephine was stunned for a second—this dragon fighting business was not a common element in her stories. Realizing she had no time to ponder this,

she began to fight with all her might.
As is the case in many dreams, Josephine
found she had a new found skill, and was
probably the best swordsman or woman in
the world!

She was making pretty good headway with
the dragon when she heard a sound from
behind her. Glancing quickly over her
shoulder, she saw another battle behind
her, boy and dragon. They were backing
towards one another.

"What are you doing?" shouted the boy.

"What does it look like I'm doing?" replied
Josephine. "I'm fighting this big dragon.
What are you doing?"

"Same," answered the boy.

"But what are you doing in my dream?"
asked Josephine, "Who are you?"

"Your dream?" laughed the boy, "Ha! I am Peter Pan."

Josephine was not sure if she heard correctly, and was getting to a crucial part of her battle. She summoned up her strength and with a great lunge, delivered the final, killing stroke to the dragon, who fell to the ground and after reducing to a pile of sand, swiftly fell through the cracks of the earth beneath their feet. Josephine felt pretty proud, and then remembered the boy behind her.

"You are not Peter Pan." She said.

"Just a minute," replied the boy. In one fell swoop, he too leveled his dragon, transforming it to a similar pile of sand that also disappeared.

The boy turned towards Josephine. She could see that he was about her age and stature and had a mischievous expression. "Yes I am." He said.

"No," started Josephine, "You may THINK you are Peter Pan, but you are not."

"Who do you THINK YOU are?" asked the boy.

"Josephine," answered Josephine.

"Who's that?" asked the boy.

"Me..." she said.

"Ugh! Dull, dull, dull, boring!" he said, "When you can THINK you are anyone in the world, you choose JOSEPHINE! I am Peter Pan."

"Okay prove it..." she thought of a good test. "If you are Peter Pan, then FLY!"

The boy smiled.

"Piece of cake," he said.

He then started to leap up and down shouting, "I can fly! I can fly! I can fly!"

But he couldn't fly. Josephine looked on, smugly.

Just then a flurry of sheep came dashing back toward them, screaming and shouting as before, but there was no Elf in sight.

"Dark Sheep! Dark Sheep!" they seemed to be screaming.

Josephine was able to stop One in his tracks.

"What is going on?" she asked.

One was out of breath and very anxious.

"The Dark Sheep is coming!" he wailed, "He has grounded all flyers and is looking for prisoners!"

"Grounded all flyers?" asked the boy.

"Yes!" replied One, "Pulled them out of the sky with his mighty woolen spell!"

"So that's why..." said the boy.

Josephine gave him a stern look and turned back towards One.

"Who is the Dark Sheep?" she asked.

The other sheep had gathered behind One, and reverently they recited, "Zero. The fallen one."

A small sheep stepped forward and began to explain, "Zero used to work with us, but the children kept skipping him during the count, and he got mad."

Another sheep stepped forward, "He was never counted so he felt he didn't count. He turned to the dark side. Now he works for the Dream Thief"

At the mention of Dream Thief all the sheep shuddered.

"The Dream Thief?" questioned Josephine and Peter.

"SHHH!" said the sheep.

"Don't say his name!" warned One, "Your thoughts might summon him!!"

"But you just---" started Josephine.

"SHHH!" said the sheep.

One glanced over his shoulder and quickly explained, "We just have a minute—the Dark Sheep is almost here. Avoid him. He will take you to the Dream Castle where darkness reigns. The Dream Thief locks up dreamers and steals their dreams in the night."

"Why does he do that?" asked Josephine.

One looked impatient, "Because he has no imagination and cannot dream himself. He destroys all dreams—he thinks that no one deserves to dream if he cannot."

"And this Zero character works for him?" asked Peter.

"Yes," replied One, "He's gone BAAAAAD!"

"BAAAAAD," repeated all the sheep.

Then with a start, the flock was off again, leaving Josephine and Peter to ponder the new information.

They did not have long to think, for as soon as the sheep took off, the dark, woolly figure of Zero came on the scene.

Zero did not look terribly menacing, but one close look at his expression told you that he had suffered a hard life and was all too eager to project his suffering onto those around him. When he saw Josephine and Peter, he smirked and threw up his hooves with a great laugh, as if casting a spell.

Josephine and Peter were not frightened at first, but when they tried to turn to escape the Dark Sheep, they found they were frozen, and unable to run.

"I can't move!" said Peter, through tight lips.

"Neither can I!" said Josephine.

"OF COURSE YOU CANNOT!" shouted Zero

in a loud, shrill voice, "YOU ARE MY PRISONERS NOW! THE NIGHTMARE IS ON ITS WAY!"

"The Nightmare?" said Peter.

As if in answer to his query, the thundering gallop of the mighty horse was upon them, shaking the ground upon which they stood. Seamlessly the mare raced towards them and lowering her mighty neck swept Josephine and Peter upon her back and continued her course.

Finding themselves able to move once more, Josephine and Peter held on to her mane for dear life, as the horse went faster and faster, finally leaving the ground and heading up deep into the night sky.

5.

WHEN JOSEPHINE awoke she found herself in total darkness, lying on a soft, but slightly prickly pile of what felt to be straw or twigs. She tried to adjust her eyes to the darkness, but was unable to do so, seeing only the blackest black she had ever experienced. She shifted slightly and tried to feel the environment around her.

Just then a voice whispered in the darkness.

"Josephine...are you there? Josephine?"

It was Peter.

"Is that you, Peter?" she asked.

"Pan," he said.

"What?" she asked.

"Peter PAN," he replied.

"Whatever," she said, "Where are you?"

"Not WHATEVER," said Peter, "Say it!"

"Okay," sighed Josephine, "Where are you, Peter PAN."

"Well, I am in this very dark place," he began.

"I know that!" she said, exasperated, "I am here too. Here—I am holding out my hand, reach for it—"

Josephine held out her hand and it was

quickly grasped by Peter. She suddenly felt less alone. Even though he was a little annoying, it was comfort to have him with her in this distressing and confusing place.

"Where do you suppose we are?" she asked.

"In the belly of a whale." He answered.

"That is ridiculous," replied Josephine.

"Not so ridiculous," he continued, "Maybe we are in a giant refrigerator, and as soon as someone gets hungry, the door will open, and the light will go on."

"That is the dumbest thing I have ever heard," said Josephine.

"Oh yeah?" said Peter, "Just because you have no imagination—we will never get out of here until you start thinking."

"THINKING?" she shouted, "That is not thinking. That is just illogical!"

"SHHHHH!" whispered a chorus of voices all around them.

The hair stood up on Josephine's neck.

"We are not alone," whispered Peter.

The darkness was beginning to slip slowly into dim light, and Josephine and Peter could barely distinguish shapes around them, and the glittering of what looked like a hundred eyes, all fixated upon them.

"Great," said Josephine, "Who are you?" she called out.

"Spiders!" chimed the chorus.

"SPIDERS!" shouted Peter, shaking.

"Hold on," said Josephine, and she addressed the group, "Spiders...as in the nice *salutations*, Charlotte's Web Spiders? Or the *Arachnophobia* type?"

The spiders conferred briefly amongst themselves before crying out, "The second kind!"

"Run!" Shouted Peter.

But it was too late. The spiders were everywhere, surrounding them, and creating great, hairy containing walls of black spindly legs.

As the darkness continued to subside, the spiders became more visible, and Josephine was surprised to see that each one had a fancy red beret perched on its head at a jaunty angle. These were spiders with style.

Before Josephine could remark on their

fashion sense, the head spider emerged from the crowd, illuminated by a giant spotlight.

"Good evening!" said the spider with a thick French accent, "I am your Nightmare Host, tonight, Monsieur Dubois. I would like to welcome you to ze Nightmare Den. Tonight's specials are—Robert, bring ze specials!"

Robert, another spider, came skittering forth, holding a menu. "But, of course!" he said.

Taking the menu, Dubois continued, "Oh yes, now where was I? We begin with Anxiety Soup, followed by a Succulent Rack of Torture, and a Raging Angry Moose."

Josephine and Peter exchanged glances and looked at the floor, not wanting to appear rude, but not wanting to partake in any of the delicacies Dubois had offered.

"Not hungry?" asked Dubois.

The two visitors shook their heads.

"Then the floor show can begin!"

The spotlight widened and Josephine and Peter were escorted to a small cabaret table within the Nightmare Den. They saw a small stage set up on one end of the space with an orchestra of earthworms and centipedes.

The music began and Josephine marveled at how the centipede seemed to be playing both a piano and a saxophone at once, when her attention was pulled to center stage by the voice of Dubois and the back-up spiders, ready to do a soft shoe floor show.

I dance.
I'm the Spider of Your Dreams.
Quel Chance!
I am bigger than I seem.
You wake up one night,
We've descended from the sky,
We've covered the walls,
And we stare you in the eye.
We're spiders, we own the night.
We're such good hiders, masters of fright.
You are not sure where we are,
We are quiet and aloof.
We never wander far,
We drop down from the roof.
La la la la la la la la!
We're Spiders, don't close your eyes!
Black, web-bound gliders, hairy surprise!
Your face, your hands, your hair,
Your walls, your rug, your bed,
We'll find you everywhere,
So get it through your head.
La la la la la la la lal!
We're spiders! We're spiders!
Nightmare spiders!
Big, black spiders!
So be afraid!
La la la!

Josephine and Peter watched with great admiration as the multi-legged creatures broke into a fancy dance, ending with a full kick-line of spider glee. As the production came to a close, the spiders began to move in on their prey from all sides and Peter and Josephine exchanged anxious looks, and held one another tightly. Josephine closed her eyes and hoped for the best, feeling the warm breath of the creatures closing in. She couldn't take it anymore.

"Stop!" she cried. In an instant the creatures disappeared, and she and Peter were left with the warm glow of the spotlight upon them. In the distance the sound of retreating hoof beats could be heard.

"Whew! Good call," said Peter. "That was close! What do we do now?

"Follow the light," said a far-off voice.

"Sounds promising," said Josephine, "Let's see where this goes."

6.

JOSEPHINE AND PETER looked up into the bright light, and just as it began to blind them, it began to move. They followed it, listening to the continuous announcement that looped over and over:

You will be entering the Dream Castle. Please keep your hands inside the car at all times. Por favor no tocan los animales peligrosos. Gracias and Thank you for riding Light Systems Transport. You will be entering the Dream Castle. Please keep your hands inside the car at all times. Por favor no tocan los animales peligrosos. Gracias and Thank you for riding Light Systems Transport.

After a long journey, the light led them through a small stone doorway, and into a large dark hall. The light swept over the floor and walls of the room revealing children, sleeping on the floor in piles of soft pillows and plush blankets, and then disappeared out a small window, leaving the room dimly lit.

Peter yawned.

"It looks like we arrived at naptime," he said, "I could use a rest myself!"

Just then, a tall shadow fell across their path-- a shadow accompanied by a long, menacing laugh. Josephine and Peter looked up into the dark sunken eyes of the Dream Thief himself!

"Yes, my children, a nap is a very good idea," he said, "Zero! Fetch some pillows for our guests."

Zero suddenly materialized with a pile of bedding in his hooves.

"But I am not tired!" protested Josephine.

"Maybe some shut-eye would be a good thing," said Peter.

Josephine pulled Peter aside, "Are you crazy? Didn't you hear what this guy does? Do you want your dreams stolen? We need to stay awake!" she whispered.

"Sure. If you believe a flock of sheep..." Peter replied, just a bit too loud.

"BAAAA!" cried Zero.

The Dream Thief laughed, "You'll be tired soon enough. Zero! Start the serenade!"

With that he turned on his heel, and was gone. Zero clashed a huge pair of sparkling cymbals together, and followed his master out of the hall.

"Serenade?" questioned Peter, "What do you suppose?"

As if in answer to his question, another

disembodied voice called out to them. This time the voice was low, steady, and mono-tone. It appeared a lecture series had begun:

The square root of 264 divided by 4 is 4 itself. The isosceles triangle, having two equal sides, can mirror itself point to point and opposite adjacent angles will be the same...

"What is going on?" asked Josephine.

The early morning dew point of any given Friday in April is directly proportionate to the perceived diameter of the moon the night before, not figuring extensive meteor activity or the crocus population for any given season.

"I think they are trying to bore us to sleep," answered Peter.

It is still under investigation if the small intestine of the early dinosaur was fully functioning or whether the hostile environment in the mouth of the creature did more digesting than we think.

"Oh it is terrible," cried Josephine, "Tune it out! Stop!"

She clapped her hands and the voice seemed to stop. Josephine breathed a sigh of relief and turned towards Peter, only to find that he had fallen into a deep, deep sleep. Josephine was overcome with panic and new found feelings of isolation.

"Peter! Peter! No, no , no. Wake up! Don't leave me!" she cried.

But her rousing efforts were in vain. No shoving or loud words could wake him. As she sunk down to the floor, defeated, next to him, she was startled by a voice from across the room. A small girl in a purple sweater had risen to her feet and was seemingly acting out a scene of her own making.

"Mom?" said the girl, "Can I go ride bikes with Sara? It's not raining that hard, and there is this purple bird that sings down by the river. It is the Yak-Yak bird, and tells the most wonderful stories."

Josephine was intrigued and approached the girl, wanting to hear more, when a boy leapt to his feet behind her with great exuberance.

"Run!!" he screamed, "Back to the trenches. I said, move it now!"

Josephine heard the wartime sounds of heavy artillery all around them, and saw the boy reach for an imaginary radio receiver.

The boy continued into the radio, "Yes Sir, they are closing in at 434 degrees. That's what I said, 434 degrees. O'Malley is down and hundreds wounded! Retreat! Retreat! Retreat!"

Josephine was impressed by this wartime drama, and was about to applaud his fine scene-work, when another red-headed girl rose to her feet beside the boy.

"I can't eat this. All my teeth are falling out," said the red-head, "Do you have any oatmeal with honey? I keep losing all my teeth."

Then the purple sweater girl was back.

"Thanks, Mom!" she said, "Yes, I'll be back at quarter to six to set the table."

One by one, the rest of the children rose to their feet acting out strange and varied scenes. It finally dawned on Josephine that all the children were dreaming, and dreaming so vividly, that they were acting out the images and dialogue in their heads. What a strange bit of entertainment for the evening!

As Josephine was just beginning to watch another installment of the war-time drama, the Dream Thief re-entered the room, this time carrying a big net on a long stick. Zero was close at his heels, carrying his magic sparkling cymbals. Josephine hid behind Peter and pretended to be asleep, keeping one eye on the menacing duo.

Dream Thief and Zero approached the

purple sweater girl, mid-story. There was a crash of cymbals, a flash of light, and a swoop of the net, and with a faint cry, the girl dropped back to the floor, exiting her dream, and slumbering deep.

"GREAT JOB, SIR!" Congratulated Zero, "YOU ARE THE TRUE MASTER!"

"File this one under MOM/BICYCLE," commanded the Dream Thief.

He glanced over at the boy in the trenches.

"Let's hold off on War Files." he said, "I don't think he's finished yet.

The two laughed to one another and exited the room.

Josephine cautiously got to her feet and walking through the forest of children acting out their own private dreams, she approached the purple sweater girl, now sleeping and breathing deeply. Josephine knelt beside her, shaking her gently. The girl awakened, groggily.

"Are you alright?" asked Josephine.

The girl looked puzzled.

"Why are you waking me up?" she asked.

"I think you were dreaming," started Josephine, but she was cut off by the girl.

"Nonsense," she said, "I don't dream!"

Josephine giggled at this.

"Of course you do," said Josephine, "I saw you! You had a dream about riding your bike to the river to hear the stories of the Yak-Yak bird."

The girl looked annoyed and said, "Uh—I really don't know what you are talking about. I live downtown in an apartment with no rivers, or bike paths. And there is no such thing as a Yak-Yak bird. I just did a report on birds, so I should know."

Josephine was taken aback and said, "But

you made it up, in your dreams, in your mind."

"Oh, so now you think I am a liar," said the girl, "That's just great. Can you let me get back to sleep, please?"

The purple sweater girl turned her back to Josephine, and swiftly fell back into a deep slumber.

"This is very strange," said Josephine.

A voice rose up from behind her, "Stranger than fiction, you might say!"

Josephine turned to see a boy in a worn baseball cap up on his feet, entertaining an imaginary crowd.

The boy continued, "Step right up, step right up, and watch the greatest balancing act of our time! Five thousand feet above a pool of fire, Alex the great balances on a tiny wire! How does he do it? No one knows. Watch my triple backflip!"

Alex did a tiny hop, and continued, "Thank you! Thank you! Wasn't that perfection? Now I will juggle three glasses of water without spilling a drop!"

Before Josephine could properly hide, the Dream Thief and Zero were back. *Crash* went the cymbals, *flash* went the light, *swoop* went the net, and *down* went Alex, with a faint, dreamless cry. Josephine cringed.

Zero turned to the Dream Thief.

"EXCELLENT," he said, "HOW SHOULD I LABEL THIS ONE?"

The Dream Thief looked thoughtful.

"Put it in the Circus Closet under DEATH DEFYING STUNTS," he said. "Anything from the new girl yet? She looks like a big dreamer.

"NOT FOR LONG!" laughed Zero, as they both exited.

Josephine ran over to where Alex was asleep on the ground and shook him vigorously.

"What is going on?" she asked.

He awakened to answer, "Well I was sleeping, and now you are waking me up."

Josephine corrected him, "No, you were dreaming."

"No, you're crazy," said Alex. "I don't dream."

"What?" asked Josephine.

"I stopped dreaming a few years ago," he said, "It's called growing up."

"But I saw you," protested Josephine, "You were doing a circus act above a pool of fire! You were magnificent!"

"Sounds like you were dreaming," said Alex as he turned over and fell back to sleep.

Josephine was overcome with worry, and

ran to Peter's side, trying once more to wake him,

"Peter, Peter!" she cried, "You must wake up! We are in great danger! Our dreams are being taken while we are asleep. You must help."

Peter jumped to his feet and exclaimed, "What is it? Is Captain Hook after you again?"

He ran around the room, as though flying and landed at Josephine's side once more.

"Tink! TInk" he cried, "Where are you? We must save Wendy again."

Josephine was beside herself, unable to pull Peter from his dream self.

"Peter! PLEASE WAKE UP!" she pleaded, "I am not Wendy, and you are not Peter Pan. We are in a very dangerous place, and we have to get out now!"

But it was too late. The Dream Thief and

Zero were upon them. In the blink of an eye, *clash*, *flash*, *swoop*, *cry*, and *fall*, and Peter lay dreamless at Josephine's feet.

"NO!! Not him!" she wailed, "Not him!"

Peter woke up and looked at her.

"What's wrong, Josephine?" he asked, calmly.

Josephine was instantly relieved.

"Oh, you do know me!" she said, "They were trying to steal your dream."

"That is silly," said Peter. "Because I don't dream."

Josephine felt her blood run cold.

"What? Of course you do. You are Peter Pan, and you were about to fly and rescue me," she said.

Peter looked at Josephine with gentle tolerance, and said, "That is sweet, Josephine, but Peter Pan is a children's book. It has nothing to do with me. You should get some rest."

This was too much. Josephine stood up and spun around to face the Dream Thief and Zero, who were looking on with amusement.

"YOU!" she said to the Dream Thief, "Why are you doing this? WHY? Why can't you allow others to see magic and envision amazing things? Why are you ruining imagination."

The Dream Thief was taken aback and rose to his full height, towering over Josephine.

"Little girl," he began, "Why are you causing such trouble? Don't you see that people get along better without troublesome dreams? Hasn't everyone told you all your life to, what was it? GET YOUR HEAD OUT OF THE CLOUDS? Where do you get the ideas for your stories, Josephine? The ones that make you different? You dream them, don't you? Aren't you tired of being different? A world without dreams is a world without disappointment."

Before Josephine could answer, a voice chimed in from behind her.

"A world without dreams is a world without possibility. Return the girl to me."

Josephine turned around to see Mr. Sand, One, and Elvis had entered the great hall.

"Sandman, we meet again," said the Dream Thief.

One spied Zero across the room and defiantly they had a quick "BAAAAA" face-off.

Mr. Sand looked across the sea of children that had returned to their sleeping spots on the floor.

"How long did you intend to go on doing this to the children?" he asked, "Stealing their imagination and---"

"And what?" interrupted the Dream Thief, "Forcing them to grow up? Is that so wrong? Don't these children deserve a world that is real and not clouded by the silly dreams in their heads? I am saving them! I am protecting them from sadness!"

Zero crashed his cymbals, and all the children sat up and focused on the Dream Thief who began an incantation:

Don't you know what you dream will not happen?
Don't you know that the world is grey and dark?
Stop pretending things will change with your vision.
Reality is harsh, and cold and stark.

Dreamers must disappear. Dreamers must run.
The path will be quite clear, when dreaming's done.
We belong to the world as it is.
Do not change, keep the world as it is.
Hours turn to days, days gather into years,
No need to change our ways,
For change invites new fears.

KILL THE DREAM

"Kill the dream?" cried Josephine

"Continue, children!" commanded the Dream Thief.

All the children, now dreamless rose their feet and began the chant:

KILL THE MUSIC. KILL THE STORIES. KILL THE FICTION. KILL THE LIES. DROP THE COLORS. AND THE MAGIC. SUPERSTITIONS. IN YOUR EYES. LIFE IS SIMPLER WHEN IT'S SOLID. WHEN IT'S FACTUAL AND GREY. NO ONE'S HURTING. NO ONE'S DIFFERENT. DISAPPOINTMENT STAYS AWAY.

Josephine and the Sandman immediately responded with a protest song of their own,

What of fire and music and hoping and dare?
They make life worth living, and make us aware
Of the places we can go, of the things we can do,
Of the love we'll come to know, of dreamers like you.

The Dream Thief waved his arms wildly and conducted the children to drown out the song of hope and good will with the droning chant. The great hall was filled with music and yelling and anger and disillusion, and the pressure mounted and filled Josephine with such sorrow that she snapped.

"OKAY!" she shouted. "Just stop the arguing. I can't take it anymore. I wanted to feel comforted by my stories. Comforted by the colors, and desires of my dreams, and I did not want to be alone in them. I get it. I have to change."

Josephine looked up at the hundreds of stars visible through the arched stone window.

"Mama," she said, "You left me without telling me how to grow up. How to say goodbye to the clouds, and accept the greyness of the world. I have learned that now without you, and I can say goodbye."

She turned back to the crowd, "Mr. Dream Thief," she began, "I don't want to be any trouble anymore. You can have my dreams. I am ready to grow up. Mr. Sandman?"

The Sandman took Josephine's hand and as

she lay down on gently on the floor, he scattered glittering stars over her resting body.

The children, including the dreamless Peter, retreated to edge of room to watch the final dream.

Josephine tossed and turned for a moment and gracefully rose to her feet. She looked around and was both sad and comforted to see the warm figure of her mother approach. Her mother took her into a great hug.

"Oh Mama!" sighed Josephine.

"Are you ready for one of our stories?" asked her mother.

"I don't think so, Mama," said Josephine. "I have to let go."

"Nonsense," replied her mother, "What do you mean?"

Josephine fought back the tears as she

mustered up the strength for this final goodbye.

"I can't live in my dreams, anymore. I have seen that the world is harsh and cold, and I must accept that. And say goodbye to you."

"Oh Josephine," sighed her mother, "It is true, you must not rely upon your dreams alone for comfort. You must find the magic that is present in daily life. And no one can take that from you. Remember—"

Her mother looked into her eyes and repeated the strains of her lullaby:

All the wonder in the world
Is not just in your head.
When you journey through the world
Please remember what I've said.
Find the giggle in the stream,
Glances between friends,
Sunsets on the ocean,
You'll see there is no end
To the magic for the dreamer who awakes.

Zero tugged on the sleeve of the Dream

Thief, who had been watching the scene with trance-like admiration.

"READY, SIR?" he asked, "SHALL WE READY THE NET?"

"No Zero," said the Dream Thief.

"WHAT?" asked Zero incredulously, "BUT THIS IS A VERY DANGEROUS MESSAGE! IT MUST BE DESTROYED."

The Dream Thief could not take his eyes off Josephine's mother.

"I am actually quite moved by what this lady says. I would like to meet her," said the Dream Thief.

Zero looked anxious.

"SIR, YOU CANNOT ENTER A DREAM," he said, "THAT IS IMPOSSIBLE."

The Dream Thief pushed Zero aside and moved towards Josephine and her mother. As soon as he got close, however, she vanished into sand with a sparkle of light, and Josephine fell to the ground. Dream over.

The Dream Thief shook Josephine.

"Little girl!" he said, "Bring her back! Bring her back again!"

Josephine sat up, a bit woozy.

"Who? What? I can't bring her back until I dream her again," she said.

"Then do it! I command you," said the Dream Thief.

The Sandman intervened, "You know you do not have the power to order dreams, you old fool!" he said, "I will keep her alive in this girl's memory and in yours if you release the other dreams and allow children to imagine again."

The Dream Thief paused for a moment, and just briefly a sense of calm and relief fluttered over his deep-set, hardened eyes.

"Sandman," he said, "You are asking me to change my entire mission in life."

"Perhaps," replied the Sandman, "But I am asking you to return hope and possibility to the world, because without that we would not be where we are today. Think of all the things we have today that came from yesterday's impossible dream."

Josephine stood up and listened closely. She suddenly heard a flutter of fairy wings, and was delighted to see the figure of her mother enter the room. Or was it the Tooth Fairy?

The Dream Thief was delighted too.

"It's you! You're back!" he exclaimed.

"I help children grow up too," she began, "But I don't steal wonder. I am a part of it. I care for their little teeth and look after them as they grow. They find disappointment along the way, but also great joy. You must allow that. Would you like to join me in my travels?"

The Dream Thief lit up with momentary joy.

"You mean free the children and leave this dark castle?" he asked, "Put the Nightmare out to pasture?"

The Tooth Fairy nodded.

"I never thought it was possible, " he continued. "This place has been so dark for so long, but it has also been home. You get used to dark places. You begin to furnish them. Could I go with you? Could you show me something different? Something light? Something with hope?"

The Tooth Fairy extended her hand and he grasped it eagerly. Her warm touch seemed to transform and invigorate him, and light flooded the castle hall.

Zero looked around in disbelief.

"DON'T DO IT, SIR," said the Dark Sheep, "WHAT WILL YOU DO? WHAT WILL WE DO? WHAT WILL HAPPEN TO ME?"

Josephine noticed that a small flock of sheep had joined One. The smallest sheep approached Zero.

"You could rejoin the flock," said the little sheep.

Zero scoffed, "RIGHT. LIKE YOU WOULD WANT ME. LOOK AT ME!" said Zero, as he pointed to the number on his bib.

The little sheep smiled.

"We can change that," she said, and she pulled a large number "1" from behind her back and affixed it to Zero's bib, transforming him into a "10".

Zero grinned and allowed a small tear of acceptance and joy to fall from his eye. The sheep cheered. Zero was back.

The Sandman turned to Elvis. "Now, let's see about getting you home," he said.

"Thank you. Thank you very much," replied the grateful Elf.

Josephine was moved by the transformation all around her. She began

to see how changeable life could be.
People come and go, and touch us deeply
and sometimes leave, but it is up to us to
make choices about who and what we want
to be. Maybe she could do this. She could,
in fact, live in a world that accepted all
kinds of people with imagination and
practicality, and differing goals and talents.
She could make her way, but she couldn't
do it alone—she couldn't isolate herself in
order to keep her memories and life
completely static. She had to grow, she had
to hold the joy of the past close, and boldly
move into the future—into a world of color
that might be different from the inside of
her own mind. It was time to open her
eyes.

7.

JOSEPHINE awoke with a jolt.

"Mama?" she called out, and then sat up and looked around the familiar surroundings.

This is my bed, this is my room...

The sunshine was streaming in her window. She had slept the whole night away.

"Josephine!" called her father from outside the door, "Are you awake? You have a visitor!"

Josephine pulled herself from the covers and loosed the bun from the top of her head, allowing her hair to fall to her shoulders. Then she remembered her essay from the night before. She reached under her pillow to retrieve it, but instead of finding her paper, she found a sparkling star shaped locket on a silver chain. Suddenly the dream came flooding back to her. She looked to the sky.

"Oh Mama," she said, "I think I am done counting stars. I know you will always be with me."

She put the locket on and started to make her bed. There was a knock at the door, and a boy slowly peeked into the room.

"Come in," said Josephine.

Much to her amazement, Josephine recognized the boy as Peter from her dream!

"Peter!" she cried out.
Peter looked perplexed.

"Uh...hi, sorry to disturb you, but we just moved in next door, and I thought I would come over and say hi," said the boy.

"It's so good to see you!" said Josephine.

"Right," said the boy, "Actually, my name is Thomas."

Thomas took in the bright surroundings of Josephine's room, "Wow! I love all the colors in your room. It's really cool."

Josephine smiled.

"Hi Thomas, I'm Josephine, " she said. "You just look like this person I knew named Peter."

"Peter Pan?" asked the boy?

"Why, yes—" started Josephine.

"That's funny," he said, "Because Peter Pan is sort of my nickname."
"Why?" asked Josephine.

"I can fly, " replied the boy with a grin.

"Really?" asked Josephine.

The boy extended his hand to Josephine and the two smiled warmly.

"You tell me," he said, "You tell me."

THE END

MUSIC

Caroline Louise Altman

Starlight

Caroline Altman

Josephine and the Sheep of Dreams

3

Sheep

Caroline Altman

Children Grow

Caroline Altman

The Oral Report

Caroline Altman

Josephine and the Sheep of Dreams

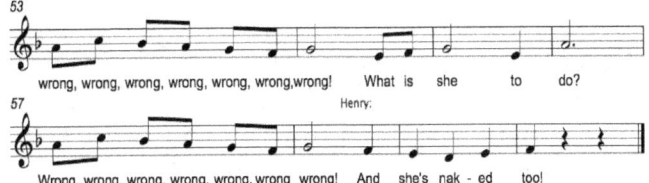

I Fell Out

Caroline Altman

Elvis:
Last Christ-mas all was swell. We load-ed up the sleigh. The us-u-al No-el did not turn out that way! We were sail - ing through the stars that night, San-ta was laugh-in' with all his might. We hit a bump in the milk - y way that sent me fly-in' right out of the sleigh! I fell out! Out! Right out of the sleigh, for me there was no Christ-mas day, I fell out! Out! Right out of the sleigh, and now I get down on my knees and pray, Won't some-bod-y get me back to the Pole? I got-ta see Sant-a, yeah, that's my goal! So lis - ten to my sad la - ment, this elf's not read-y for re - tire ment! He fell out! Out! Right out of the sleigh, for him there was no Christ-mas day, He fell out! Out! Right out of the sleigh, and

Sheep:

Josephine and the Sheep of Dreams

Colors

Caroline Altman

Josephine and the Sheep of Dreams

Music in the Trees

Caroline Altman

The Spider of Your Dreams

Caroline Altman

Kill the Dream

Caroline Altman

Don't youknow what you dream will not hap pen? Don't youknow that the world is grey and

dark? Stop pre-tend-ing things will change with your vi sion. Re - al - i-ty is harsh and cold and

stark! Dream-ers must dis-ap- pear, dream-ers must run. The path will be quite clear

when dream-ing's done._____ We be-long to the world as it is._____ Do not

change, keep the world as it is._____ Hours turn to days, days gath-er in-to years.

No need to change our ways, for change in-vites newfears. Kill the dream._____

What of fire and mus-ic and hop-ing and dare? Theymake live worth liv-ing and

make us a-ware of theplac-es we can go, of thethings we can do, of the love we'll come to know, of

Josephine and the Sheep of Dreams

dream-ers like you.

Kill the music. Kill the stories. Kill the fiction. Kill the lies.
Drop the colors. And the magic. Superstitions. In your eyes.
Life is simpler when it's solid. When it's factual and grey.
No one's different. No one's hurting. Disappointment stays away.

What of fire and mus-ic and hop-ing and dare? They

make live worth liv-ing and make us a-ware of the plac-es we can go, of the things we can do, of the

love we'll come to know, of dream-ers like you.

Star light star bright

first lit - tle star I see___ to-night I wish I may, wish I might,

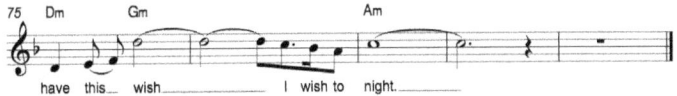

have this___ wish_____ I wish to night._____

Dreamers Tonight

Caroline Altman

The Musical

Josephine and the Sheep of Dreams, the Musical
is available for production. Featuring a flexible cast
of 13, with expandable chorus, this delightful 50
minute family musical features lively melodies, and
a poignant and humorous script.
www.lyricabellaproductions.com

ABOUT THE AUTHOR

A musical theater professional, Caroline Louise Altman is a singer, actor, composer, director, educator, and Founding Artistic Director of Lyricabella Productions. Her award winning musicals and TYA pieces include *Whiskers! The Musical of the Velveteen Rabbit; Josephine and the Sheep of Dreams; Kiss the Frog; The Snow Queen: Splinters of Ice;* and the operatic anti-bullying touring show, *How Andy Found His Voice.* Collaborative musicals include *Moments of Truth; Not Without Our Women;* and *Alice in Cyberland.* Her performing career has taken her all over the U.S. and Europe, and has garnered her a San Francisco Bay Area Theater Critics Circle Award and a Shellie Award for Contribution to the Performing Arts.

Her love of storytelling and fiction led her to create *The Indy Stories: One Feline's Quest for Cultural Adventure* which combines her three loves: art, travel, and seeing the world through the eyes of a small furry creature. Her first book, *Indy at the Opera*, was published in April, 2014. Caroline lives in Oakland, California, with her husband, Matt. Learn more about Caroline at:

www.carolinealtman.com

Caroline Louise Altman